D1103351

Published by Ladybird Books Ltd
27 Wrights Lane London W8 5TZ
A Penguin Company
2 4 6 8 10 9 7 5 3 1
LADYBIRD and the device of a Ladybird are trademarks of Ladybird Books Ltd

© Disney/Pixar MM
Adapted from Walt Disney Pictures' and Pixar Animation Studios **Toy Story 2**
Mr. Potato Head® is a registered trademark of Hasbro, Inc. Used with permission.
© Hasbro, Inc. All rights reserved. Slinky® Dog © James Industries.

All rights reserved. No part of this publication may be reproduced,
stored in a retrieval system, or transmitted in any form or by any means,
electronic, mechanical, photocopying, recording or otherwise,
without the prior consent of the copyright owner.

Printed in Italy

Disney • PIXAR

TOY STORY 2

Ladybird

Woody, Andy's favourite toy, was getting ready to go to Cowboy Camp with Andy later that day. He was pleased when Andy came in to play with him and Buzz.

But the game got a little rough, and disaster struck – Woody's arm tore!

"Oh no!" cried Andy. "Mum, you have to fix Woody right away!"

"I'll mend him later," she replied, and she put Woody up on the mending shelf. Andy was very upset – he had to leave for camp without his best cowboy friend.

As Woody sadly watched Andy leave, he heard a cough nearby. It was Wheezy, the toy penguin, stuck behind some books.

"Why didn't you call for help?" Woody asked.

"Why bother?" asked Wheezy. "We'll all end up in the same place." He pointed out the window to the lawn below, where Andy's mum was putting up a "YARD SALE" sign.

"Yard sale alert!" shouted Woody. The toys rushed to hide, but it was too late for Wheezy.

"Bye, Woody," the little penguin called as Andy's mum carried him out to the garden.

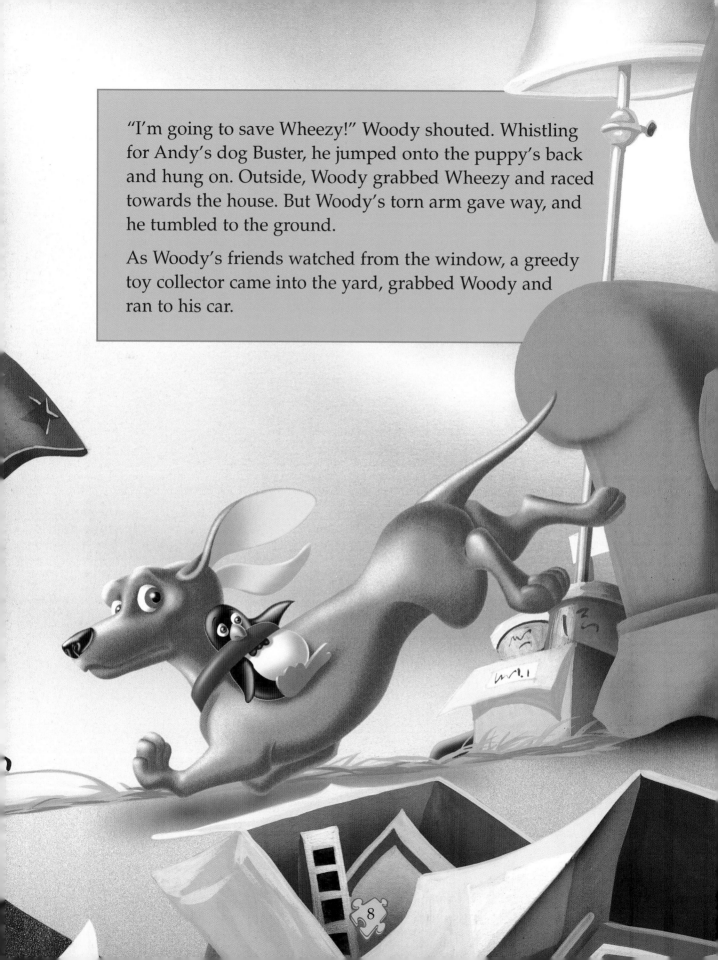

"I'm going to save Wheezy!" Woody shouted. Whistling for Andy's dog Buster, he jumped onto the puppy's back and hung on. Outside, Woody grabbed Wheezy and raced towards the house. But Woody's torn arm gave way, and he tumbled to the ground.

As Woody's friends watched from the window, a greedy toy collector came into the yard, grabbed Woody and ran to his car.

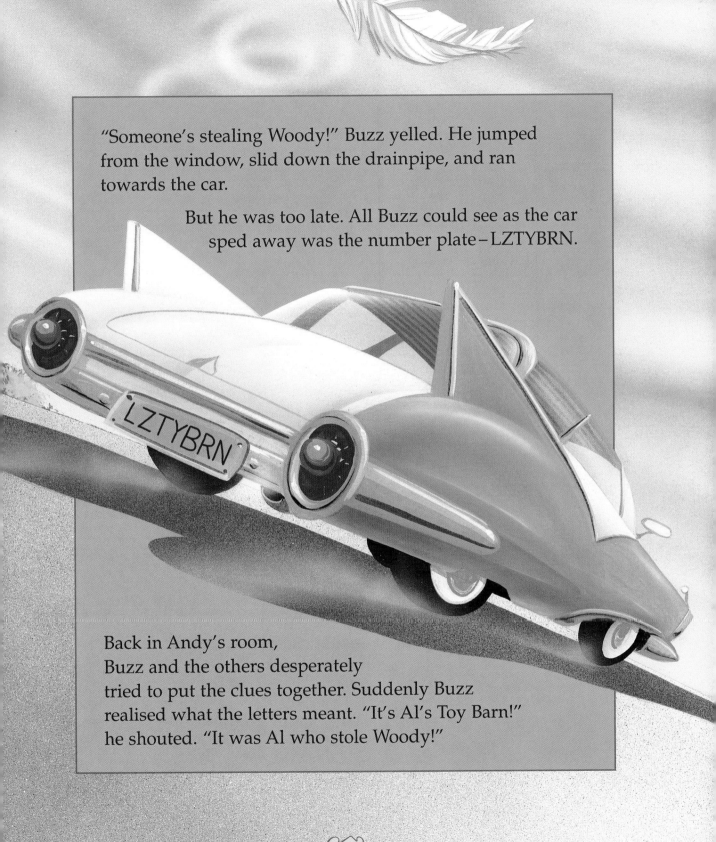

"Someone's stealing Woody!" Buzz yelled. He jumped from the window, slid down the drainpipe, and ran towards the car.

But he was too late. All Buzz could see as the car sped away was the number plate – LZTYBRN.

Back in Andy's room, Buzz and the others desperately tried to put the clues together. Suddenly Buzz realised what the letters meant. "It's Al's Toy Barn!" he shouted. "It was Al who stole Woody!"

Buzz was right. At that moment, Al was setting Woody down in his apartment. "You're going to make me big money!" he chuckled.

As soon as Al was gone, Woody tried to escape. But before he could get very far, a toy horse and a cowgirl doll popped out of their boxes to welcome him. "Howdy, Woody!" exclaimed Jessie the cowgirl.

"How do you know my name?" Woody gasped.

Woody's ROUNDUP

SAYS 6 DIFFERENT THINGS

PROSPECTOR

Hey Howdy Hey!

POSEABLE TALKING DOLL • WITH PICK AXE

WR TOYS

POSEABLE TALK
Woody's ROUNDUP

"Let's show you who you really are," said a Prospector doll.
Jessie switched on a television set.

"It's Woody's Roundup!" a cheerful voice on the TV
announced. "Starring Jessie, the yodelling cowgirl... Stinky Pete
the Prospector... Bullseye the horse... and Sher-r-r-riff Woody!"

Woody couldn't believe it – he had once been a TV star!
"Now you're part of a very collectable set – us!" the Prospector
explained. "Al is selling us to a museum in Japan."

"I don't want to go to a museum," Woody insisted.
"I want to go back to Andy."

"But if you go, we'll be put
away in storage for ever,"
Jessie said sadly.

15

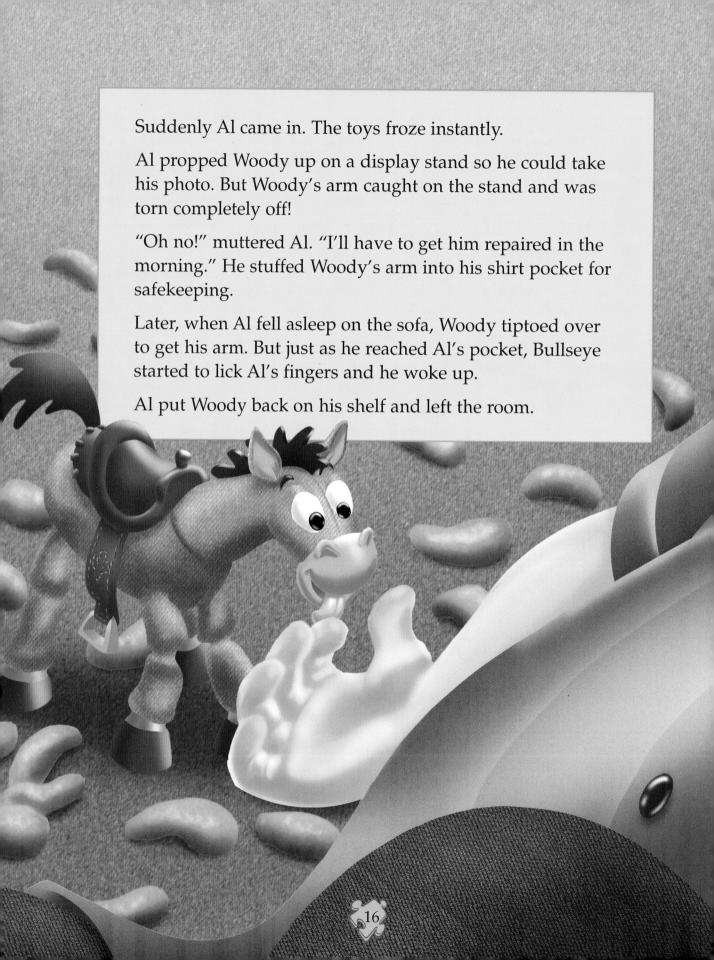

Suddenly Al came in. The toys froze instantly.

Al propped Woody up on a display stand so he could take his photo. But Woody's arm caught on the stand and was torn completely off!

"Oh no!" muttered Al. "I'll have to get him repaired in the morning." He stuffed Woody's arm into his shirt pocket for safekeeping.

Later, when Al fell asleep on the sofa, Woody tiptoed over to get his arm. But just as he reached Al's pocket, Bullseye started to lick Al's fingers and he woke up.

Al put Woody back on his shelf and left the room.

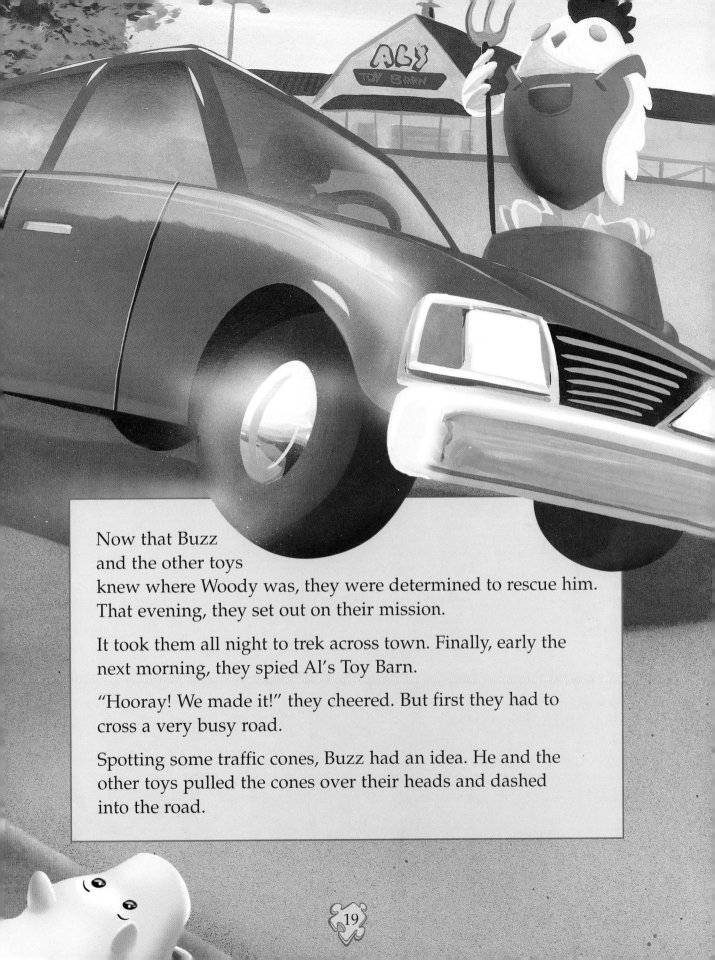

Now that Buzz
and the other toys
knew where Woody was, they were determined to rescue him.
That evening, they set out on their mission.

It took them all night to trek across town. Finally, early the
next morning, they spied Al's Toy Barn.

"Hooray! We made it!" they cheered. But first they had to
cross a very busy road.

Spotting some traffic cones, Buzz had an idea. He and the
other toys pulled the cones over their heads and dashed
into the road.

"Drop!" Buzz shouted, and everyone stopped.

SCREE-EE-EECH! A car swerved round the cones.

"Go!" Buzz yelled. "Drop! Go! Drop!" Buzz shouted commands until, at last, the toys made it across the road.

"Good job, troops!" said Buzz. "Excellent covert manoeuvring. Now let's keep moving."

In the road, cars and lorries were smashing into each other, but the toys ignored them. They just kept hurrying towards Al's Toy Barn.

At the same time, the Toy Repairer arrived at Al's apartment. He opened his amazing toy repair kit and set to work. Before long, Woody looked brand new.

"Well, I'm all ready to go home to Andy now," said Woody, when the Toy Repairer had gone.

"Andy will outgrow you one day," Jessie said, "just like my little girl outgrew me. You'll end up in a charity shop, just like I did."

"It's true, Woody," the Prospector added. "You'll be better off in a museum."

"Maybe you're right," Woody said thoughtfully. "I think I'll stay after all."

Inside Al's Toy Barn, Woody's friends stood speechless. Above them towered hundreds of shelves stacked with thousands of toys, all newer and shinier than they were.

"How will we ever find Woody in here?" Rex whined.

"Rex, you and Slinky take the action figure aisles," Buzz commanded. "Mr Potato Head and Hamm, you take preschool to board games. I'll take the perimeter. We'll all meet at the back."

As his friends scattered, Buzz noticed a strange green light in a nearby aisle. When he went to investigate, he found an awesome Buzz Lightyear display—featuring a new Buzz Lightyear. This New Buzz had an amazing utility pack, complete with grappling hook, string and magnetic radials.

"I could use that!" thought Buzz, moving towards the new toy.

"Hi-yaah!" the New Buzz yelled, grabbing Buzz and throwing him to the floor. The two space heroes tangled and wrestled, and the New Buzz finally won. He fastened Andy's toy into a box and crammed it on a shelf.

27

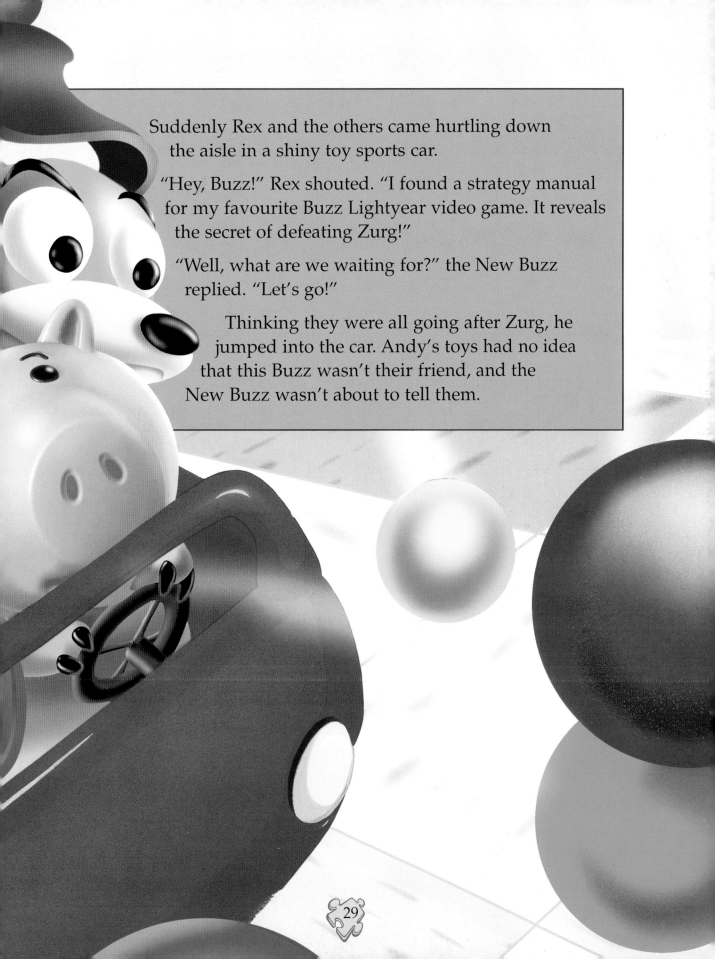

Suddenly Rex and the others came hurtling down the aisle in a shiny toy sports car.

"Hey, Buzz!" Rex shouted. "I found a strategy manual for my favourite Buzz Lightyear video game. It reveals the secret of defeating Zurg!"

"Well, what are we waiting for?" the New Buzz replied. "Let's go!"

Thinking they were all going after Zurg, he jumped into the car. Andy's toys had no idea that this Buzz wasn't their friend, and the New Buzz wasn't about to tell them.

Suddenly the toys
heard a voice. It was coming from
Al's office. As Al talked on the phone
to his buyers in Japan, the toys clambered
out of the car and into his open briefcase.

"I'll be on the last plane tonight with Sheriff
Woody and the entire set," Al promised the buyers.

"I've just closed the deal of a lifetime," he gloated
as he hung up the phone and grabbed
his briefcase.

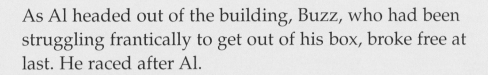

As Al headed out of the building, Buzz, who had been struggling frantically to get out of his box, broke free at last. He raced after Al.

Pushing over a huge stack of toy boxes to trigger open the automatic doors, Buzz ran towards Al's apartment. But he failed to notice that behind him, one toy box lay stuck in the shop doorway.

BANG! BANG! The automatic doors opened and closed, hitting the box again and again. At last the box tore open, and the evil Emperor Zurg slowly emerged!

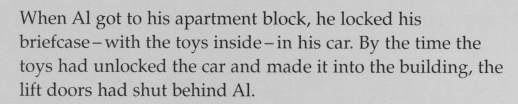

When Al got to his apartment block, he locked his briefcase – with the toys inside – in his car. By the time the toys had unlocked the car and made it into the building, the lift doors had shut behind Al.

Using the magnets from his utility belt, the New Buzz found a way up through a vent in the lift shaft. He dropped a line down for the others, and they all began to climb.

Suddenly, the lift came up below them, catching them on its roof. As the toys rode the lift to the top of the building, the real Buzz caught up and was now clinging to the bottom!

CRASH! The toys
smashed into Al's flat
through a vent.

"We're here, Woody!" the New Buzz
yelled, rushing up to Bullseye.

"That's not Woody," said Andy's toys suspiciously.
"And if you don't know who Woody is... then
you're not Andy's Buzz. Where is he?"

"Right here!" Buzz announced, stepping into the room.
"I'm the real Andy's Buzz—look!" He lifted his foot to show
them Andy's name written on the bottom. The other toys
knew at once that this was their friend.

37

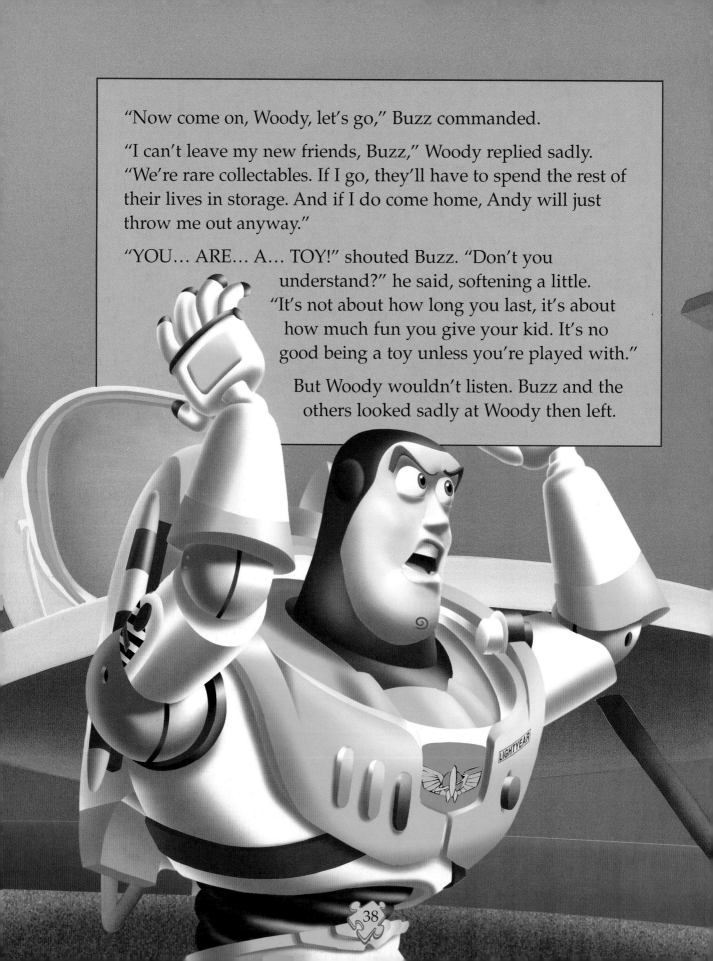

"Now come on, Woody, let's go," Buzz commanded.

"I can't leave my new friends, Buzz," Woody replied sadly. "We're rare collectables. If I go, they'll have to spend the rest of their lives in storage. And if I do come home, Andy will just throw me out anyway."

"YOU… ARE… A… TOY!" shouted Buzz. "Don't you understand?" he said, softening a little. "It's not about how long you last, it's about how much fun you give your kid. It's no good being a toy unless you're played with."

But Woody wouldn't listen. Buzz and the others looked sadly at Woody then left.

39

Woody turned back to his TV programme. "You've got a friend in me," the TV Woody sang to a little boy.

Suddenly Woody missed Andy terribly. He knew that he'd made a mistake–a big one.

"Buzz! Wait!" he cried. "Come on," Woody called to Jessie and Bullseye. "We have to catch up with my friends!"

But as they headed for the vent, the Prospector blocked their way. And just at that moment, Al came into the apartment, scooped the toys into his suitcase and set off for the airport!

Luckily, Buzz had heard Woody. "Guys!" Buzz shouted. "Woody changed his mind! We have to get him—follow me!"

As the toys raced towards the lift shaft, an ominous black-robed figure with gleaming eyes suddenly rose up before them. It was Zurg, standing on the roof of the lift!

With an evil laugh, Zurg attacked. Buzz and the New Buzz fought back bravely.

While Rex hid in terror, Zurg loomed over the New Buzz and raised his arm to strike.

"I have to see what's happening!" Rex exclaimed, suddenly turning round. THWACK! His tail knocked Zurg off the roof.

"AAAAAAAAH!" Zurg screamed as he fell.

"I defeated Zurg!" Rex shouted.

Zurg was gone, but Woody still needed help. The toys peered into the lift and saw Al with his suitcase. Woody was inside.

Quickly the toys formed a chain, with Slinky at the end. Stretching his coils, Slinky managed to unlatch the case. But the Prospector quickly yanked Woody out of reach.

The lift stopped and Al stepped out. Slinky dangled forlornly in mid-air for a moment, then crashed to the floor with his friends on top of him.

Waving goodbye to the New Buzz, Andy's toys raced out of the lift and through the lobby doors.

46

Al's car was just pulling away. Suddenly, Mr Potato Head spotted a Pizza Planet van nearby. The toys clambered aboard. Buzz climbed onto a pile of pizza boxes to get to the steering wheel.

"Slink, you take the pedals. Rex, you navigate. Hamm and Potato, operate the levers and knobs," he commanded.

The van lurched forward and swerved onto the road. "Go left... I mean right... no, no, I mean your right!" Rex shouted as the van zigzagged through the traffic.

The van came to a halt at the airport's loading zone. Al was already hurrying inside.

The toys jumped into a pet carrier and chased after him. When Al's case went onto the baggage conveyor belt, the pet carrier, propelled by tiny legs, hopped on as well.

Inside the baggage area, the toys jumped out. Hundreds of bags, boxes and suitcases were speeding past them. How would they ever find the right one?

Buzz wasn't about to give up. "Split up and start looking," he told the others. He began running up and down the conveyor belts, searching for the case that had Woody inside.

"I think I've found it!" Buzz shouted when he saw a green case zipping past. Quickly he unlatched it and looked inside.

POW! A fist shot out and punched Buzz. It was the Prospector. He climbed from the case, swinging his pickaxe.

Scrambling out of Al's bag, Woody climbed over to where Buzz and the Prospector were fighting. Together Woody and Buzz stuffed the Prospector into a passing rucksack.

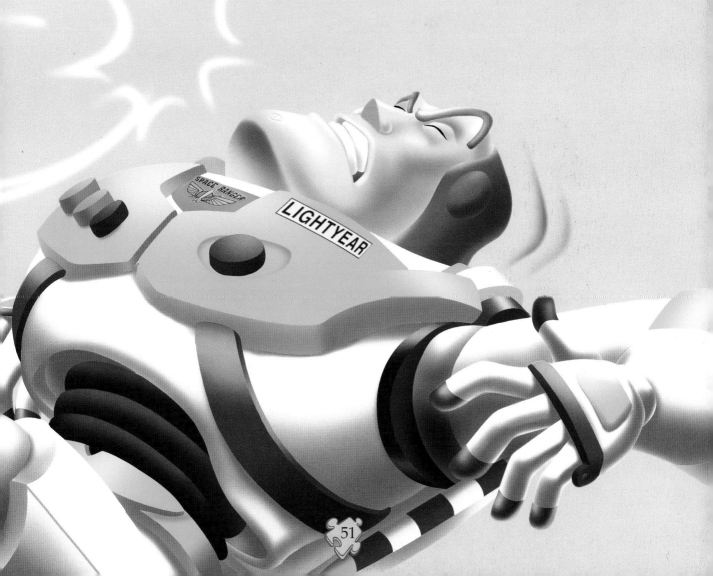

Buzz and Woody knew there was no time to waste. They had to save Bullseye and Jessie!

But Bullseye had already managed to struggle free from the case. Woody flung himself onto the little horse's back, pulled Buzz up behind him and galloped after the baggage train.

"Watch this, Buzz!" Woody shouted. "I saw it on my TV show!" Balancing on Bullseye's back, he gave a loud "YA-HOO!" and leapt onto the speeding train.

But before Woody could reach Jessie, the train stopped, and a baggage handler tossed Al's case into the cargo hold.

Woody couldn't let Jessie down. He jumped into a golf bag just as it was being loaded onto the plane.

"Oh, Woody, I'm so glad to see you!" Jessie exclaimed when Woody opened Al's bag.

"We're not safe yet," Woody said grimly. "And we don't have much time left." He led Jessie through the cargo hold to the escape hatch just over the plane's wheels. But the plane was already beginning to move onto the runway.

Jessie and Woody looked down. If they jumped and fell under the enormous wheel, they'd be crushed. But if they didn't try, they'd never make it off the plane and back to Andy.

As the two toys climbed down towards the wheel, Jessie slipped. Woody reached out to grab her, when – RRRRI-I-I-IP!

"My arm is tearing!" he shouted. His grip weakened, and he slipped from the edge of the escape hatch.

"Woody, help!" cried Jessie, dangling just inches above the churning wheel. Thinking quickly, Woody yanked his pullstring as far as it would go and lassoed Jessie with it.

At that moment, Bullseye and Buzz galloped up. "Jump, Woody, jump!" shouted Buzz. Woody grabbed Jessie and they jumped safely onto Bullseye's back.

"Yeeeee-haaaah!" cried Woody. "Now we can go home!"

A short time later, Andy arrived home. He rushed upstairs, burst into his room and grabbed Woody from the shelf.

"Howdy, pardner!" he exclaimed. "Boy, did I miss you."

Then Andy saw Jessie and Bullseye and to their delight he played with them all afternoon.

Woody and Buzz smiled. They knew there was nothing like being a toy—especially one that lives in Andy's room.